This Book Belongs to:

PETAL

....

FOR MY DARLING SOPHIE, IN HONOR OF YOUR WONDERFUL,
HILARIOUS CHILDHOOD TEMPER —MF

Tundra Books, an imprint of Penguin Random House Canada Young Readers,
a division of Penguin Random House of Canada Limited

LIBRARY AND ARCHIVES CANADA CATALOGUING IN PUBLICATION
Title: Petal the angry cow / Maureen Fergus ; illustrated by Olga Demidova.
Names: Fergus, Maureen, author. | Demidova, Olga, illustrator.
Identifiers: Canadiana (print) 2020021604X | Canadiana (ebook) 20200216058
ISBN 9780735264687 (hardcover) | ISBN 9780735264694 (EPUB)
Classification: LCC PS8611.E735 P48 2021 | DDC jC813/.6—dc23

Published simultaneously in the United States of America by Tundra Books of
Northern New York, an imprint of Penguin Random House Canada Young Readers,
a division of Penguin Random House of Canada Limited

Library of Congress Control Number: 2020936841
Edited by Samantha Swenson
Designed by Terri Nimmo
The art in this book was rendered in Adobe Photoshop with a pinch of love.
The text was set in ITC Zemke Hand

Printed in China

www.penguinrandomhouse.ca

1 2 3 4 5   25 24 23 22 21

Penguin
Random House
tundra | TUNDRA BOOKS

PETAL
THE
ANGRY
COW

MAUREEN FERGUS

OLGA DEMIDOVA

tundra

In many ways, Petal was everything
you could want in a cow.

She was a hard worker,

a talented artist

and a great dancer.

She had a keen mind
and a kind heart.

Unfortunately, Petal also had a temper.

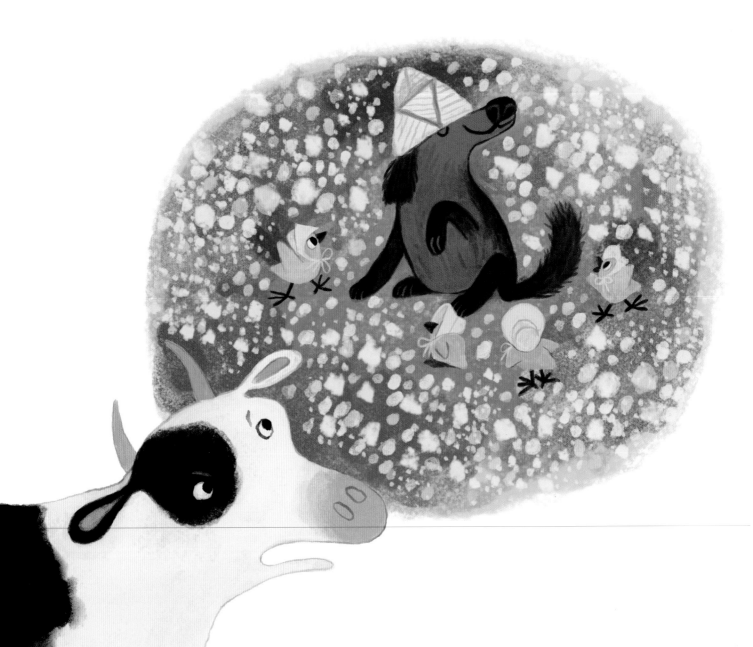

If the dog borrowed her stuff
without asking, she'd try to bite him.

If the pigs played a practical joke on her, she'd try to kick them.

If the chickens teased her,
she'd shout bad words at them.

And if the sheep cut in front of her at
the trough line . . .

LOOK OUT!

As you can imagine, Petal's temper
frequently got her into trouble.

She received long, boring lectures.

She was forced to apologize,
even to the chickens.

And, of course,
she got Time-Outs.

Sometimes, she used her Time-Outs to consider
what she might have done differently.

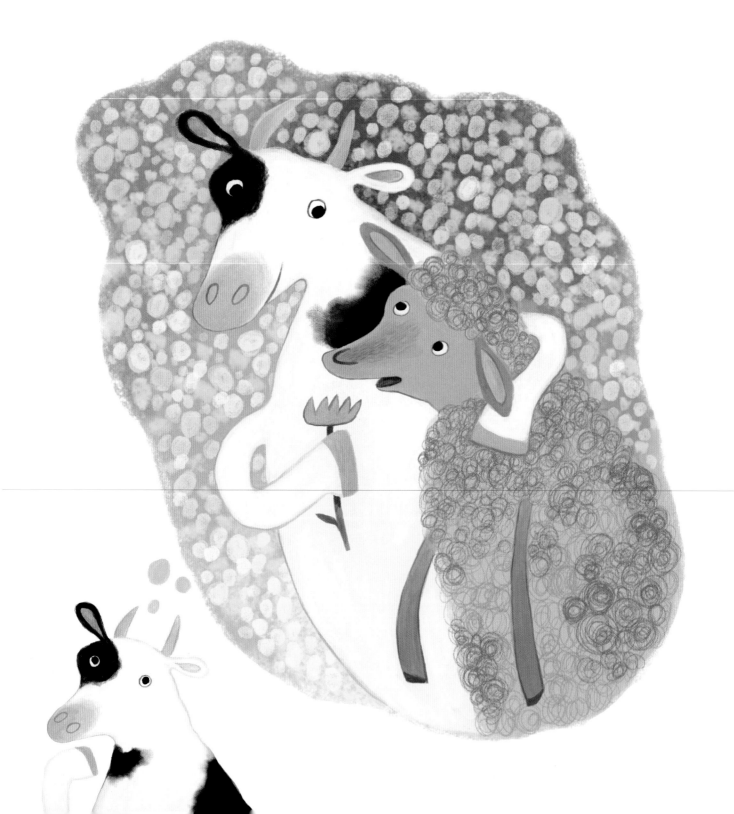

Mostly, though,
she plotted revenge.

One morning, the farmer made an announcement:

"Tomorrow, we're going on a field trip to the water park.

On our way home, we'll stop for pizza and ice cream."

All the animals cheered!

As the horse was
jumping for joy,
she accidentally
landed on
Petal's hoof.

It hurt so much that Petal almost started crying!

"WATCH IT, DUMMY!"

she hollered.

"Petal!" gasped the farmer.
"Apologize or I will have to give you
a consequence!"

Petal didn't want a consequence, but she
was still so angry that she couldn't stop
herself from stomping and shouting.

In the barnyard, there was a moment of stunned silence. Then the farmer said, "Petal, until you learn to control your temper, I'm afraid you won't be joining us on any field trips."

Wailing with anguish, Petal galloped across the
meadow and collapsed at the edge of the pond.

At length, a beautiful swan glided over.
"What's wrong?" he asked.

"My temper got me in trouble again!" sobbed Petal.

"My temper never causes me problems,"

said the swan. "Would you like to see why?"

"Oh, yes!" said Petal.

The swan accompanied Petal back to the barn.
The other animals were so charmed by
his grace and majesty that they invited him to
play in the Go Fish tournament.

Things went well until the swan lost his first game.

Clearly upset, he took several deep breaths . . .

Then he leapt up, knocked over
the card table and screamed,

"I HATE
THIS
STUPID
GAME!"

"See?" said the swan.
"I didn't want to keep playing, and now
the game is over. No problem!"

Even though the other animals weren't quite as charmed by the swan anymore, they later allowed him to join them at the craft table.

Things went well until one of the chicks accidentally scribbled on his drawing.

In a menacing voice,

the swan counted to ten . . .

Then he started shrieking and pelting crayons at the poor chick.

"See?" said the swan.
"I wanted to get back at that
little birdbrain and I did.
No problem!"

After that, none of the other animals wanted the swan
to come to Story Time, but Petal persuaded them to give him
one more chance.

Things went well until the farmer said he was going to
read the story the sheep had chosen instead of the one
the swan had chosen.

The swan got up and stalked into the barn.

Petal hoped that he was just taking a moment to calm down.

After that, none of the other animals wanted the swan
to come to Story Time, but Petal persuaded them to give him
one more chance.

Things went well until the farmer said he was going to
read the story the sheep had chosen instead of the one
the swan had chosen.

The swan got up and stalked into the barn.

Petal hoped that he was just taking a moment to calm down.

Once the swan got over his tantrum, Petal said,

"If you want to be our friend, you need to start

acting like a friend. No screaming. No shrieking —"

"No thanks!" griped the swan.

As Petal watched him fly away, she thought about how he'd looked and sounded when he'd lost his temper.

She thought about what she'd said to him about acting like a friend.

And she knew it was time to take her own advice.

So after lunch, when the horse accidentally slammed the barn door on Petal's tail again, Petal took several deep breaths and then asked her to please be more careful in the future.

And during naptime, when Petal cut the cheese and the pigs wouldn't stop laughing, Petal counted to ten and then ignored them until they lost interest.

And that evening, when the dog arrived at the corn roast wearing Petal's favorite beret, Petal walked away until she'd calmed down. Then she quietly said, "If you don't put my beret back, I'm going to tell the farmer."

Petal climbed into bed that night feeling proud and happy.

"Controlling my temper wasn't easy," she told the farmer.

"Many things worth doing aren't easy," he replied.

"Now go to sleep, Petal — you've got a big day tomorrow."

"I do?" she said.

"Yes," said the farmer
with a smile. "You do."

AND SHE DID.